PILLYCOCK'S SHOP

Story by

MARGARET MAHY

Pictures by

CAROL BARKER

INTERNATIONAL

Franklin Watts, Inc.
575 Lexington Avenue
New York, New York 10022

Text and illustrations copyright © 1969 Franklin Watts, Inc.

Published in the United States by Franklin Watts, Inc.,
and in Great Britain by Dobson Books Ltd.

Library of Congress Catalog Card Number: 74-76743

Printed in Austria

One day Teddy took the babies for a walk down the road which ran, gray and gravelly, past the fine brown gate which Teddy's father had made. The pine trees saw him go, and nudged one another.

"There goes Teddy!" they said, and all the little pine cones in rows on the branches squeaked, "Where? Where? Where? Where? Are those *his* babies?"

The babies weren't Teddy's at all, and as a matter of fact he was not pleased at even having to look after them. Their names were Valentine and Penelope, but they were called Val and Penny for short. As Teddy wandered along, pushing the big pram and thinking about eeling in the creek, what should he see but a shop where no shop had ever been before, snuggled in beside the trunk of a fallen tree.

It was small,
very small for a shop.
Indeed, its door was
just high enough
to let Teddy in,
and a grown-up man
would have had
to crawl through
on his hands and
knees. Its funny
window frame and
door were highly
polished and shone
like well-rubbed
mahogany, a deep
reddish-brown, and
its window was as
clear as air.

Around the window
and the door someone
had carved grapevines,
and leaves, birds, and
bunches of grapes.
But as Teddy looked
closely, he saw that
there were faces
peeping at him from
behind the leaves—
carved wooden faces—
and some of them
were not very pleasant
with their cunning eyes,

and greedy, grinning mouths. Over the door the name was carved . . . PILLYCOCK'S SHOP!

Teddy looked in the window and found that the shop was full of delights . . . little cages of silver wire and ivory with crickets hopping inside them, a clock, with two tiny figures that danced when it struck the hour, a sea horse in a glass bowl, lengths of silk embroidered with butterflies and cobwebs, earrings of emeralds, a fan of peacock's feathers, and a great, glowing tiger skin. Teddy couldn't help himself. He pushed the pram through the little low doorway and into the shop.

It was much larger inside than Teddy had thought it would be. The counter was long and brown, and did not go all the way down to the floor as most counters do. Instead it stood on four thin, bony feet with crooked toenails, and when Teddy came in, it scuttled sideways on these feet, and the little faces carved at its corners grimaced or spat, catlike, at him.

But the man behind it patted the counter and said, "Be quiet now, steady, it's only a customer."

He was a strange fellow, this man behind the counter, yellowish altogether, with slanting yellow eyes and a sallow skin. He wore a saffron-colored turban, and his dark beard was arranged in neat rows of small curls. The smock he wore had once been white, but was now faded and discolored, and over it he wore a strange necklace of golden bells and bangles. Indeed the man himself had a faded and discolored look, from his goatish beard down to his grimy, sandaled feet. He grinned at Teddy.

"Do you like my shop?" he asked. He tried to grin at the babies, but they didn't like him, and began to grizzle and sniff.

"Sweet children!" the man murmured to Teddy. Then he said, "There are two rules. You can buy only one thing—that's the first rule."

He paused a moment, then went on speaking, in a low, intense tone: "And the second rule is that you must buy it by sundown, because the shop goes away then. Once the sun is down, I go down too, as it were. Also"—he added in a mutter, as if he didn't really want Teddy to hear this part—"if you want to change anything you buy, you must do it by sundown, too, or I take your money forever . . . But you won't *want* to change anything, of course," he continued in a loud voice, "for few people have the chance to buy from a shop such as mine."

"Pillycock's Shop!" Teddy said.

"Yes, Pillycock's Shop!" the man echoed with a shriek of rusty dusty laughter that obviously hadn't been used for years. Before him on the counter lay four piles of silver coins, and one of gold. There was also a shell, and a stone ring. The man saw Teddy looking at these things.

"It is mine—yes, all of it," he boasted. "Mine! . . . Here's a Phoenician coin, very rare. This one comes from Cathay, and this golden one from Damascus in the days of its power. The stone ring is the first coin I ever earned—in Neolithic times long, long ago. Nineveh and Babylon, Luxor and Athens, yes and Rome too—in all these great old cities men have bought from Pillycock's Shop. It is an ancient come-by-chance shop, and only appears once in five hundred years."

Teddy thought of these great old cities whose names were so strange to him. "You must be very old," he said.

The man just grinned at him with pointed teeth. Teddy thought, "This is a wicked man." But he forgot this when he looked around the shop and saw the wonderful things there.

There was a picture of a ship in a gilded frame, and as Teddy stared, the wind blew and the foam flew, and the ship rose and fell over the waves. Then it came into a wharf by a walled city where hundreds of gaily dressed people met it, waving banners and cheering as the gangplank went down—and out came a parade of crowned kings and queens in purple and gold.

"Would you like to buy that picture?" the man asked. Teddy tore his eyes away from it, shook his head and looked elsewhere. The man picked up a little box and opened it. Immediately music began and a rabbit appeared offering a plate with a whole watermelon on it, cut into pink, sweet slices.

"The rabbit is the servant of whoever owns the box," the man said slyly. "Is *that* what you'd like?" Teddy shook his head. The rabbit vanished and the music stopped.

"Oh well!" The man sighed. He took out a ribbon hung with bells and shook it. As the bells rang a tiny, clear, imperious sound, out from each bell at each ring flew a tiny silver bee. The tiny glistening swarm clustered on the table a moment, then cleared and flew back into the bells. But on the table where they had settled was a small honeycomb.

"Try it!" the man said. So Teddy did, and it tasted delicious.

But Teddy didn't want the bells. Everything in the shop seemed too mysterious and wonderful to really belong to him.

Then, without warning, Teddy found the thing he wanted. In a small brass cage crouched a small monkey. It looked so real it was hard to believe it was only a painted tin creature.

It wasn't much bigger than a man's hand, and it was brown. Teddy looked at it, delighted with the odd little cap it wore, and with its wise, sad eyes. But as he stared he discovered something about it different from every other monkey he had ever seen. Sprouting from its shoulders were two little brown wings, folded over each other like patient hands.

"Now that monkey," said the man, "is of a very unusual kind. It tells stories to earn its living. Don't you?" he added to the monkey. He turned a little gold key in its back.

"Yes—oh, *yes-s!*" the monkey answered with a sad and tinny, wheezing sigh.

"I'd love to have it," Teddy said yearningly, "but I don't have any money . . . not any money at all."

The man looked very shrewd and sly.

"It only costs a penny," he said wheedlingly. Teddy emptied out his pockets, but there was no penny hiding there.

"Are you sure you haven't a penny of *any* kind?" asked the man in a very meaningful voice, and suddenly Teddy thought of the girl-baby Penelope, called Penny.

"That girl-baby is called Penny," he said.

"Well, it's just luck, isn't it?" cried the man, flinging up his hands. "You have a penny, after all!"

Teddy knew that the girl-baby Penny wasn't his, but he agreed to give her to the man in exchange for the monkey in the cage. You may think this was very wrong of Teddy, but he intended to go home and get a real penny-coin from his mother, then hurry back to give it to the man, and get the baby Penny back. That was truly what he meant to do, so he didn't think it was wrong to exchange a baby for a monkey.

So a minute later there Teddy was, outside Pillycock's Shop with the monkey cage in one hand, pushing the pram with the other. The pram felt much lighter with only one baby in it, and strangely enough Teddy didn't like the lightness of it. He felt very uneasy at the thought of leaving Penny with that grubby, pointy-toothed man. Never mind! He would be back soon, and he had the monkey with him, here in his very hand. Yet Teddy didn't feel as pleased about this as he had felt a minute ago. Instead he felt small and troubled inside. He looked at the monkey. He turned its key a little.

"Hello!" he said softly to it, but it didn't answer. It just bared its teeth at him and sneered. At this moment Val began to whimper, missing Penny, and he sounded so small and alone in the large pram that Teddy stopped ance more, uncertain quite what to do. And then he noticec the shadows, the long dark shadows, creeping across the road. In a flash he realized that it was nearly sunset. Sunset! At sunset Pillycock's Shop would vanish, with its peculiar shopkeeper and with Penny too! Teddy turned the pram around and ran back, quickly, quickly!

Thank goodness, the shop was still there. He didn't waste time looking at it from the outside, yet somehow it seemed to him that it wasn't as shiny and bright as it had been. And when he got inside—well! he stood aghast, for all he could see was ruin, decay, downfall, and havoc. The shelves were sagging and damp. All the fascinating things on them were withered or crumpled, rusting, broken, and dirty. Only the counter was the same, scuttling sideways again as he came in, and, yes, the man still sat behind it. But he was covered in cobwebs as if spiders had been spinning over him for a thousand years or more.

"Well!" he said, and his voice sounded angry and even more distressed and cracked than before.

"I want the baby Penny back, and to leave this monkey!" cried Teddy angrily.

The man grinned. He put the monkey's cage back in the corner, and said, "If you can *find* her by sunset, I'll be only too glad to change things for you."

But where *was* Penny? Teddy searched wildly, pulling open boxes and finding only dirt, moth-eaten fragments, and hurrying, hairy spiders. Opening cupboards, he discovered nothing beyond rotting shelves, and huge, yellow-toothed rats, and even a few grim, gnawed bones.

"Pillycock's Shop!" the man said gloatingly, "Pillycock's Shop!" and he laughed and laughed.

Then, as Teddy searched, the man played a music box, and its tiny, tinny, tinkling tune was enough to drive one mad as it went on, over and over and over and over again.

"You have only three minutes left," the man said at last.

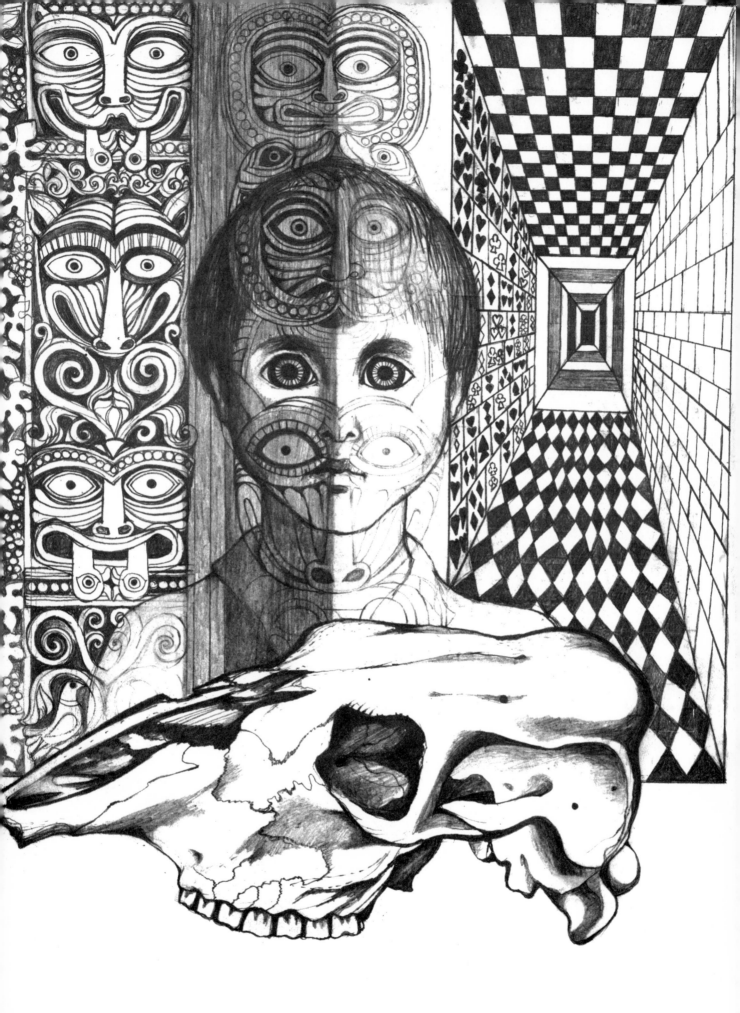

Teddy looked up desperately and as
he did so, he saw something he hadn't
noticed before. On the counter were the
piles of silver, and the pile of gold,
the shell, and the stone ring all
covered in dust. But beside them was a
bright, new penny and there was no
dust on it at all. Teddy was sure it
hadn't been there before.

"Give me my penny!" he cried out,
pointing. The man snatched up the penny
in his long, strong fingers.

"All in good time!" he said sharply.
"What makes you think that it's yours?"

Teddy knew the man hoped to keep
him guessing and talking until the three
minutes had gone, but now he was really
anxious and alert. Besides, he knew a
bit about magic.

"It's mine, and you know it!" he
shouted. "Give it to me, or the sun
won't ever go down until you do."

The man snarled, and looked with
horrible furious eyes at him. Then he
flung the penny to the ground, and
where it fell, there was Penny—
Teddy's own girl-baby Penny!
Hurriedly he gathered her up and
bundled her into the pram . . . there
was no time to waste!

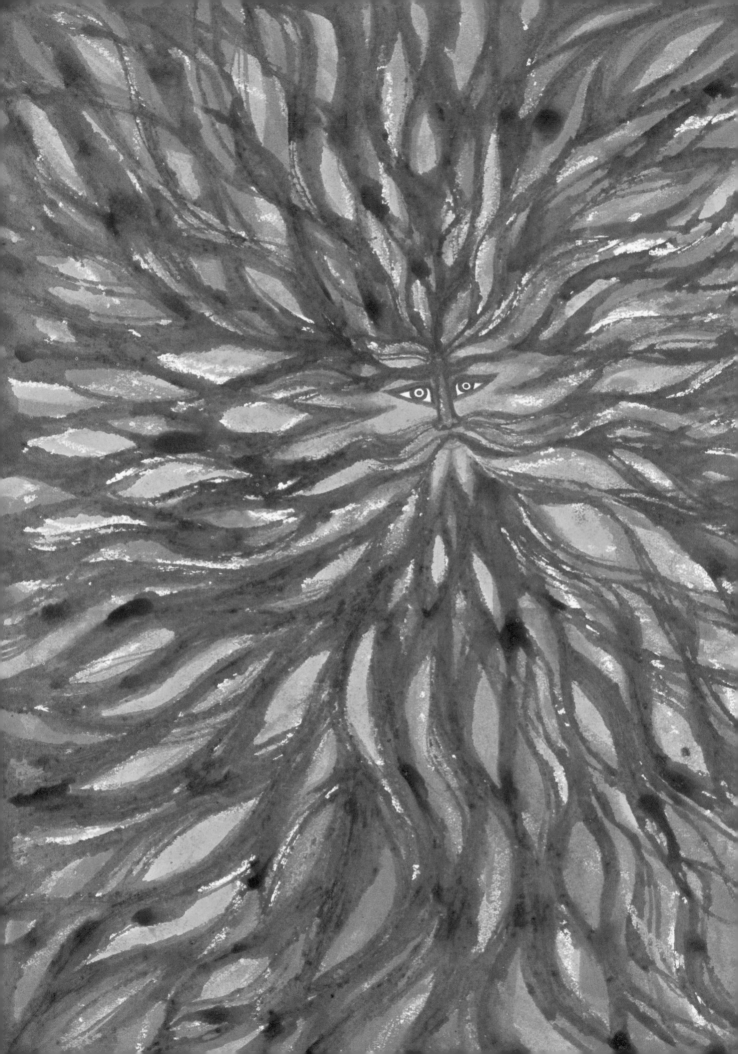

"Thank you!" he said politely as he pushed the babies out of the shop, but all the man behind the counter did was to give a curious, desolate, hungry cry and out of the corner of his eye, Teddy saw that this very strange fellow was slowly crumpling and changing into yellow dust.

The next minute Teddy was out of the shop—and just as well too, for the sun set and Pillycock's Shop vanished like a blown-out candle flame, as silently, as secretly as it had come. Where did it go to? Now, who can tell? Like the call of a bird, like the toll of a bell, it was gone, it was gone.

Never would the quiet country places or the cities of men see it again for five hundred years.

Teddy pushed the pram up the road again. Grayness had settled on everything when the sun vanished, and Teddy felt very tired and weak and thankful as he suddenly saw the windows of his home, above on the hillside, blossom out into warm, welcoming light as if someone had pinned marigolds to the white walls of the house.

So Teddy quickened his steps
happily, thinking to himself that,
after all, he would gladly exchange
Pillycock's Shop and all its many
wonders for tea with the babies
at his own house.